Robert Williams Buchanan

Napoleon Fallen

A lyrical drama

Robert Williams Buchanan

Napoleon Fallen
A lyrical drama

ISBN/EAN: 9783744796705

Printed in Europe, USA, Canada, Australia, Japan

Cover: Foto ©Andreas Hilbeck / pixelio.de

More available books at **www.hansebooks.com**

NAPOLEON FALLEN

A Lyrical Drama

BY ROBERT BUCHANAN

STRAHAN & CO., PUBLISHERS
LUDGATE HILL, LONDON
1871

TO THE PROPHETS AND MARTYRS.

O Prophets! that look forward, searching slow
   The future time for signs, what see ye there?
What faint gleams of portent come and go?
   On what, with lips like quivering leaves, and hair
   Back blowing in the whirlwind, do ye stare
So steadfast, and so still? O speak, and tell—
Is the Soul safe? Shall the sick world be well?
   Will morning glimmer soon, and all be fair?
O Martyrs! all ye see this day is sad,
   And in your eyes there swim the fatal tears,
But on your brows the Dawn gleams cold and hoar.
I too gaze forth, and my heart grows glad—
   I catch the comfort of the golden years—
I know the Soul is safe for evermore.

PREFATORY NOTE.

In reading this Napoleonic Play, or Lyrical Drama, or Dramatic Poem (I know not which is the fit title), it should be remembered that we lack as yet the proper foreground for the contemplation of the chief character. Fortunately, the subject, if treated with any ordinary skill, will be always gaining instead of losing that artistic distance which many think so necessary; while, on the other hand, it is likely to secure certain elements of real strength from the mere fact of its being based on contemporary events. Of course, it is more than ordinarily open to abuse, for ardent politicians who would let me have my own way with Tiberius or Peter the Great, or even Bonaparte, are certain to rate me roundly if I disagree with them about Louis Napoleon.

The man who here soliloquises may not be the real Napoleon, but I believe there is some justification for my portrait. After all, truth is one thing, and dramatic truth is another. If my play possess verisimilitude, no critic has a right to object to it because he himself would have conceived the chief character differently.

One final word. I desire to say that I have nowhere in the following pages expressed my own political opinions.

ROBERT BUCHANAN.

NAPOLEON FALLEN

οὐκ . . . . . σε φῶ βεβουλεῦσθαι καλῶς·
. . . . ἦσθα μηκετ' ὢν ἢ ζῶν τυφλος.
      .   .   .   .
    παντα μὴ βουλου κρατειν·
και γὰρ ἃ κρατησας οὔ σοι τῷ βίῳ ξυνεσπετο.
              SOPH. ŒD. TYR.

b

SPEAKERS.

NAPOLEON III. OF FRANCE.

AN OFFICER OF THE IMPERIAL STAFF.

A ROMAN CATHOLIC BISHOP.

A PHYSICIAN.

MESSENGERS.

FIRST GERMAN CITIZEN.

SECOND GERMAN CITIZEN.

GERMAN CITIZEN'S WIFE.

CHORUS OF REPUBLICANS.

CHORUS OF SPIRITS.

SCENE.—*The Chamber of a Health-Resort in* Cassel.
TIME.—1873, *shortly after the Surrender of Sedan.*

.˙. There are certain places anachronisms in time. That is to say, the Fall of Rome, and the proclamation of the French Republic, only reaches Wilhelmshöhe about the same time as the news of the capitulation of Paris, so as to make it possible to unite to the action of the drama which focuses at once all these historic incidents.

ERRATA.

Page 12, last line but one, *for* " Weissemberg," *read* " Wer-
senburg."

Page 51, line 1, *read*

" While Trochu, from the presidential seat,"

While russet trees to left and right

Snaring the rosy shafts of light

Shade them to silver, till they glow

There on the roof of the château

Gleaming bright ruby !

B

German Citizens walking in the Gardens without.

FIRST CITIZEN.

How fine it is to lounge in talk
Together, down this long green walk:
While russet trees to left and right
Snaring the rosy shafts of light
Shade them to silver, till they glow
There on the roof of the château
Gleaming bright ruby!

B

SECOND CITIZEN.

Not too near—
The place is private.

FIRST CITIZEN.

Didst thou hear
The news?   Another glorious blow
For Fatherland!

SECOND CITIZEN.

To-night at five
I saw the courier arrive,
Bringing the news to him who waits
Yonder.—O he may thank the fates
He sits so snug, the man of sin!—

How cunningly, before the end,
The Snake contrived to save his skin!

FIRST CITIZEN.

Thou art too hard upon him, friend.
He saw that all his cards were played,
And so, to save more bloodshed, strayed
Into the cage.

SECOND CITIZEN.

A cage, indeed!

FIRST CITIZEN.

What could he do?

SECOND CITIZEN.

Could he not die?

FIRST CITIZEN.

Die?   Sentiment!   If I were he
I'd bless the stars which set me free
From that foul-hearted Whore's embrace,
France, with her fickle painted face.
Better in Germany to dine,
Smoke one's cigar, and sip one's wine ;
And in good time, like most, no doubt,
Who have worn their wicked members out,
Repent, and be absolved, and then
Die in one's bed, like smaller men !

SECOND CITIZEN.

Thou cynic!

FIRST CITIZEN'S WIFE.

Dost thou think that he
Is happy?

FIRST CITIZEN.

Why not? . . Possibly,
My dear, 'tis something after all
To know the worst that can befall;
To know, whatever joy or sorrow
Fate is preparing for the morrow,
It cannot make more dark the lot
Our hearts to-night. Happy! Why not?
Happy as most of our poor kind.

WIFE.

He has so much upon his mind!

FIRST CITIZEN.

A woman's thought;—but hark to me,
And take this for philosophy—
Beyond a given amount of pain,
The spirit suffers not a grain.
What stuff we humble folk are taught
Of monarchs and their weight of thought!
Why, thou and I, and Jack and Jill,
Feel just as much of good and ill,
Of life and strife, of thought and care,
As he who sitteth musing there!

SECOND CITIZEN.

I saw him walking, yesterday.
He is much aged of late, they say—

He stoops much, and his features are
Gray like the ash of the cigar
He smokes for ever.

FIRST CITIZEN (to WIFE).

Come, my dear,

Let's home! 'Tis growing chilly here ;
So!—take my arm.   Yes, I contend
It matters little in the end
If one be beggar, priest, or king—
The whip's for all—the pang, the sting !
Dost thou remember—canst forget ?
When all our goods were seized for debt,
In Friedberg ?   Claim was heap'd on claim—
Blow came on blow—shame follow'd shame ;
And last, to crown our dire distress,
Thy brother Hans' hard heartedness.
Think you I felt a whit less sad,
Less thunderstruck, less fierce, less mad,

Than yonder melancholy Man,
When, through the dark cloud of Sedan,
He, as a star that shoots by night,
Swept from his sphere of lonely light,
And at the feet of Wilhelm lay
Glow-worm-like, in the garish day
Of conquest?   Well, well! wait and see—
I rose again, and so may he.
The world is but a play, tho' ye
Dear creatures take it seriously :
I cannot pity from my heart
The player of the Monarch's part,
For at the worst he never knows
The famish'd Body's bitter throes.
I pity more with all my soul
The filler of the Soldier's rôle,
Who feels the ball, and with a groan
Sinks in the bloody ranks unknown,

And while the far-off cannon cries,

Kisses his sweetheart's hair, and dies!

[*Exeunt.*

Enter, within the Château, NAPOLEON and a
PHYSICIAN.

PHYSICIAN.

The sickness is no sickness of the flesh,

No ailment such as common mortals feel,

But spiritual; 'tis thy fiery thought

Drying the wholesome humour of the veins,

Consuming the brain's substance, and from
thence,

As flame spreads, thro' each muscle, vein,
and nerve,

Reaching the vital members. If your High-
ness

Could stoop from the tense strain of great
    affairs
To books and music, or such idle things
As wing the weary hours for lesser men!
Turn not thine eyes to France; receive no
    news ;
Shut out the blinding gleam of battle ; rest
From all fierce ache of thought ; and for a
    time
Let the wild world go by.

NAPOLEON.

                    Enough, old friend :
Thine is most wholesome counsel. I will
    seek
To make this feverish mass of nerve and
    thew,
This thing of fretful heart-beats,

Fulfil its functions more mechanically.
Farewell.

PHYSICIAN.

Farewell, Sire. Brighter waking thoughts,
And sweeter dreams, attend thee ! 	*[Exit.*

NAPOLEON.

All things change
Their summer livery for the autumn tinge
Of wind-blown withering leaves. That man
	is faithful,—
I have not my life from his cold palm for
	years,
And I believe, so strong, do use and wont
Foster such natures, he would die to serve
	me.

Yet do I see in his familiar eyes

The fatal pain of pity.   I have lain

At death's door divers times, and he hath
    slowly,

With subtle cunning and most confident
    skill,

Wooed back my breath, but never even then,

Tho' God's hand held me down, did he regard
    me

With so intense a gaze as now, when smitten

By the mail'd hand of man.   I am not dead!

Not dying! only sick,—as all are sick

Who feel the mortal prison-house too weak

For the free play of Soul!   I eat and drink—

I laugh—I weep, perchance—I feel—I think—

I still preserve all functions of a man—

Yet doth the free wind of the fickle world

Blow on me with as chilly a respect

As on a nameless grave.   Is there so sad

A sunset on my face, that all beholding
Think only of the morrow?—other minds,
Other hearts, other hands?   Almighty God,
If I dare pray Thee by that name of God,
Strengthen me! blow upon me with Thy
    breath!
Let one last memorable flash of fire
Burst from the blackening brand!—

                        Yes, sick—sick—sick;
Sick of the world; sick of the fitful fools
That I have played with; sick, forsooth, of
    breath,
Of thought, of hope, of Time.   I staked my
    Soul
Against a Crown, and won.   I wore the
    Crown,
And 'twas of burning fire.   I staked my
    Crown

Against a Continent, and lost.   I am here ;
Fallen, unking'd, the shadow of a power,
Yet not heart-broken—no, not heart-broken—
But surely with more equable a pulse
Than when I sat on yonder lonely Seat
Fishing for wretched souls, and for my sport,
Although the bait was glorious gifts of earth,
Hooking the basest only.   I am nearer
To the world's heart than then : 'tis bitter
      bread,
Most bitter, yea, most bitter ; yet I eat
More freely, and sleep safer.   I could die
      now :
And yet I dare not die.

                              Maker of men !
Thou Wind before whose strange breath we
      are clouds
Driving and changing !—Thou who dost
      abide

While all the crowns on all the heads of
    kings
Wither as wreaths of snow!—Thou Voice that
    dwellest
In the high sleeping chambers of the great,
When council and the feverish pomp are
    hush'd,
And the dim lamp burns low, and at its side
The sleeping potion in a cup of gold :—
Hear me, O God, in this my travail hour!
From first to last, Thou knowest—yea, Thou
    knowest—
I have been a man of peace: a silent man,
Though loving, most ambitious to appease
Self-chiding sense of mental littleness,
A builder in the dark of temples fair
Where men might meet together not for
    praise,
A pleasure-roofed height for simple men—

In all, a man of peace.   I struck one blow,
And saw my hands were bloody ; from that
    hour
I knew myself too delicately wrought
For crimson pageants ; yea, the sight of pain
Sicken'd me like a woman.   Day and night
I felt that stain on my immortal soul,
And gloved it from the world, and diligently
Wrought the red sword of empire to a scythe
For the swart hands of husbandmen to reap
Abundant harvest.—Nay, but hear me swear,
I never dreamed such human harvests blest
As spring from that red rain which pours this
    day
On the fair fields I sowed.   Never, O God,
Was I a warrior or a thing of blood ;
Always a man of peace :—in mine ambition
Peace-seeking, peace-engendering ;—till that
    day

I saw the half-unloosen'd hounds of War

Yelp on the chain, and gnash their bloody
   teeth,

Ready to rend mine unoffending Child,

In whose weak hand the mimic toy of empire

Trembled to fall. Then feverishly I
   wrought

A weapon in the dark to smite those hounds

From mine imperial seat; and as I wrought

One of the fiends that came of old to Cain

Found me, and since I thirsted gave to me

A philtre, and in idiocy I drank:

When suddenly I heard as in a dream

Trumpets around me silver tongued, and saw

The many colour'd banners gleam i' the sun

Above the crying legions, and I rode

Royal before them, drunk with light and
   power,

My boy beside me blooming like a rose

To see the glorious show. Yet God, my God,
Even then I swear the hideous lust of life
Was far from me and mine ; nay, I rode forth,
As to a gay review at break of day,
A student dazzled with the golden glare,
Half conscious of the cries of those he ruled,
Half brooding o'er the book that he had left
Open within his chamber. "Blood may flow,"
I thought, " a little blood—a few poor drops,—
A few poor drops of blood : but they shall
     prove
Pearls of great price to buy my people peace ;
The hounds of War shall turn from our fair
     fields,
The cannon shall become a trump of praise,
And on my son a robe like this I wear
Shall fall, and make him royal for all time !"
O fool, fool, fool ! What was I but a child,
Pleased beyond understanding with a toy,

Till in mine ears the scream of murther'd
France

Rang like a knell. I had slain my best
beloved !

The curse of blood was on mine hands
again!

My gentle boy, with wild affrighted gaze,

Turn'd from his sire, and moaned; the hounds
of War

Scream'd round me, glaring with their pitiless
eyes

Innumerable as the eyes of heaven ;

I felt the sob of the world's woe ; I saw

The fiery rain fill all the innocent air ;

And, feeble as a maid who hides her face

In terror at a sword flash, conscience-struck,

Sick, stupefied, appalled, and all alone,

I totter'd, grasped the empty air,—and
fell."

CHORUS.

STROPHE I.

Ah woe! ah woe!
How art thou fallen, Man of Mysteries!
Is this the face, are these the subtle eyes,
Kings sought in vain to fathom, and to know?
    O Man of Mysteries,
    O thou whom men deem'd wise,
Call not on God this day—His hand hath
    struck thee low.

ANTI-STROPHE I.

Call not on God, but listen.
Yea, with thy soul's ears, listen! The earth
    groans,

The thunder roars, swords flash, blue lightnings glisten!

Hark! those are human moans!

List! the sharp rattle of the fiery hail,

The splashing rain of blood! Dost thou turn
pale?

Who wrought this? who atones?

What, Thou the people's Shepherd? Look, and
see:

Thy fields are darken'd with a blood-black
pall;

Thy farms are ruinous; in the granary,

Where golden wheat should be,

The wounded lambs are gather'd as they fall.

O Man of Mysteries,

Hearken unto their cries;—

Call not on God this day—'tis now too late
to call.

Strophe II.

Yet, if thou darest, pray.   Thou canst not tell
How prayer may bring thee gain ;—
And with thy prayer say thou these words as
    well :—
" Soon falls the house mark'd with the cross
    of Cain ! "
O man, with secret hands thou didst prepare
A Pleasure-house most rare,
A beauteous Temple magically built,
So that thy people gladden'd unaware
And wandering therein forgot thy guilt,
And drank the amorous ditties woven there
To lutes of lechers and their lemans fair ;
And all glad things were welcome in thy
    sight
Save the glad air of heaven; all things
    bright

Save the bright light of day ; and all things
sweet
Save country-textured Truth and Honesty :
All these thou didst abolish from thy Seat,
Because these things were free.

 Thou call on God this day—
 Thou call to the Most High—
Who asked Hell's blessing then, and let
God's gifts go by !

ANTISTROPHE II.

Pray yet, and heark. This Temple where thy
name
Was floated forth by silver choirs of Fame,
This Pleasure-house of nations, this abode
Of strange enchantments, in due time became
An outrage and a shame,
 Abominable in the eyes of God ;

For all the beauteous things within the
    place
Were witchcraft : all its glory was a lie ;
Not one true angel but perceived it base—
There was no gift of grace
But such as bawds may sell and gold can
    buy ;
Nay, even Art and Music, each with face
Averted, passed in tears.   Thereon a cry
Went up against thy marvellous work and
    thee
From the throats of all things free.
And o'er thy fields the desolating horde
Like to a swarm of locusts rose and
    spread !
The lightning of the Lord
Struck at thy glorious Temple, and it fled
Like vapour before sunlight !   The green
    sod

Is bloody where it stood and fair feet trod.

    Fallen with thee it lies,

    And it shall ne'er arise.

How should God bless thy work? Thou did'st

    not build to God.

Enter a BISHOP.

NAPOLEON.

Speak out thy tidings quickly,

How fares it with the Empress and my son?

BISHOP.

Well, Sire. They bid thee look thy fate in the

    face,

And be of cheer.

NAPOLEON.

Where did'st thou part with them?

BISHOP.

In England, Sire, where they have found a
    home
Among the frozen-blooded islanders
Who yesterday called blessings on thy brow,
And now rejoice in thy calamity.
Thus much thy mighty lady bade me say,
If I should find thee private in thy woe :—
With thy great name the streets are garrulous ;
Mart, theatre, and church, palace and prison,
Down to the very commons by the road
Where Egypt's bastard children pitch their
    tents,
Murmur "Napoleon ;" but, alas ! the sound
Is as an echo that with no refrain,
No loving echo in a living voice,
Dies a cold death among the mountain
    snow.

NAPOLEON.

Old man, I never looked for friendship there,
I never loved that England in my **heart**;
That 'twas by such a sampler **I believed**
To weave **our France's fortunes thriftily**
With the **gold tissues of prosperity.**

BISHOP.

Ah, Sire, if I dare speak—

NAPOLEON.

Speak on.

BISHOP.

Too much

France goes to that cold isle of heretics

Turn'd from thy throne for use and precedent;
Too little did they look, and that too late,
On that strong rock whereon the Lord thy God
Hath built His Holy Church.

NAPOLEON.

                    Something of this
I have heard in happier seasons.

BISHOP.

                    Hear it now
In the dark day of thine adversity.
O Sire, by him who holds the blessed Keys,
Christ's Vicar on the earth for blinded men,
I do conjure thee, hearken—with my mouth,
Tho' I am weak and low, the Holy Church
Cries to her erring son!

NAPOLEON.

Well, well, he hears.

BISHOP.

Thou smilest, Sire. With such a smile, so grim,
So bitter, didst thou mock our blessed cause
In thy prosperity.

NAPOLEON.

False, Bishop, false!
I made a bloody circle with my sword
Round the old Father's head, and so secured him
Safe on his tottering Seat against the world,
When all the world cried that his time was come,

What then? He totter'd on. I could not
   prop
His Seat up with my sword, that Seat being
   built,
Not on a rock, but sand.

BISHOP.

               The world is sick
And old indeed, when lips like thine blas-
   pheme.
Whisper such words out on the common air,
And, as a child,
Blow thy last hopes away.

NAPOLEON.

         Hopes, hopes! What hopes?
What knowest thou of hopes?

Bishop.

Thy throne was rear'd

Nay hear me, Sire, in patience to the end;
Not on the vulgar, unsubstantial air
Which men call Freedom, not on half consent
Of unbelievers—tho', alas! thou hast stoop'd
To smile on unbelievers—not on lives
That saw in thee one of the good and wise,
Not wholly on the watchword of thy name;
But first on this—the swords thy gold could
    buy,
And most and last, upon the help of those
Who to remotest corners of our land
Watch o'er the souls of men, sit at their
    hearths,
Lend their solemnity to birth and death,
Guide as they list the motions of the mind,
And as they list with darkness or with light

Appease the spiritual hunger.   Where

Had France been, and thou, boasted Sun of
    France,

For nineteen harvests, save for those who
    crept

Thine agents into every cottage door,

Slowly distilling thro' each vein of France

The vital blood of empire ?   Like to slaves

These served thee, used thy glory for a charm,

Hung up thine image in the peasant's room

Beside our blessed saints, and cunningly,

As shepherds drive their sheep unto the fold,

Gather'd thy crying people where thy hand

Might choose them out for very butchery.

Nay, more ; as fearful men may stamp out
    fire,

They in the spirits of thy people killed

The sparks of peril left from those dark
    days,

When France, being drunk with blood and
    mad with pain,
Sprang on the burning pyre, and all her
    raiment
Burning and streaming crimson in the wind,
Curst and denied her God. They made no scar,
Yea in the very name of Liberty,
A net of Satan's set to ... the soul
From Christ and Christ's salvation: in their
    pains
They welded the soft clay of popular thought
In a new ... 'd semblance yet more cunningly;
... a peasant heir of his own fields,
And ... that own'd a house,
And ... a man or woman who had saved,
But when some wild voice shriek'd out
    "Liberty!"
Trembled ... the ... and ...
Already ...

Clutch'd at his little store. These things did
    they,
Christ's servants serving thee,; they were as
    veins
Of iron binding France to thee, its heart,
Throbbing full glorious in the capital.
And thou, O Sire, in thine own secret mind
Knowest what meed thou hast accorded
    them,
Who, thy sworn liegemen in thy triumph-
    hour,
Are still thy props in thy calamity.

NAPOLEON.

Well ; have you done ?

BISHOP.

Not yet.

NAPOLEON.

What more?

BISHOP.

Look round
This day on Europe, look upon the World,
Which, like a dark tree o'er the river of Time,
Hangeth with fruit of races, goodly some,
Some rotten to the core. Out of the heart
Of what had seem'd the sunset of the west,
Rises the Teuton, silent, subtle, and sure,
Gathering his venom slowly like a snake,
Wrapping the sleepy lands in fold by fold;
Then springing up to stab his prey with fangs
Numerous as spears of wheat in harvest time.
O, he is wise, the Teuton, he is deep
As Satan's self in perilous human lore,

Such as the purblind deem philosophy!

But, be he cunning as the tempter was,

Christ yet shall bruise his head; for in himself

He bears, as serpents use,

A brood of lesser snakes, cunning things too,

But lesser, and of these many prepare

Such peril as in his most glorious hour

May strike him feebler than the wretched
    worms

That crawl this day on the dead lambs of
    France.

Meantime, he to his purpose moveth slow,

And overcomes. Note how, upon her rock,

The sea-beast Albion, swollen with idle
    years

Of basking in the prosperous sunshine, rolls

Her fearful eyes, and murmurs. See how
    wildly

The merciless Russian paceth like a bear

His lonely steppes of snow, and with deep

    moan

Calling his childless young, casts famished eyes

On that worn Paralytic in the East

Whom thou of old didst save. Call thou to

    these

For succour; shall they stir? Will the sea-

    beast

Budge from her rock? Will the bear leave

    his wilds?

Then mark how feebly, in the wintry cold

Old Austria ruffles up her plumage, Sire,

Covering the half-heal'd wound upon her

    neck;

See how on Spain her home-bred vermin feed,

As did the worms on Herod; Italy

Is a dove-cote by a battle-field,

Abandon'd to the kites of infamy;

Belgium, Denmark, and Helvetia,

Like plovers watching while the wind-hover
Strikes down one of their miserable kind,
Wheeling upon the wind, cry to each other;
And far away the Eagle of the West,
Poised in the lull of her own hurricane,
Sits watching thee with eyes as blank of love
As those grey seas that break beneath her feet.

NAPOLEON.

This is cold comfort, yet I am patient. Well?
To the issue! Dost thou keep behind the
    salve
Whose touch shall heal my wounds? or dost
    thou only,
As any raven on occasion can,
Croak out the stale truth, that the day is lost,
And that the world's slaves knee the con-
    queror?

BISHOP.

Look not on these, thy crownèd peers, for aid,
But inward.   Read thy **heart**.

NAPOLEON.

It is a book
I have studied **somewhat deeply**.

BISHOP.

In thine heart,
That the cold lips might **sneer, the dark brow
frown,**
Wert thou not **ever one believing God?**

NAPOLEON.

I have believed, and do believe, in God.

BISHOP.

For that, give thanks to God.   He shall up-
    lift thee.

NAPOLEON.

How?

BISHOP.

  By the secret hands of His great Church.
Even now in darkness and in scenes remote
They labour in thy service; one by one
They gather up the fallen reins of power
And keep them for thy grasp; so be thou
    sure,
When thou hast gather'd round about thy soul
The Robe of Holiness, and from the hands
Of Holy Church demandest thy lost throne,
It shall be hers to give thee.

NAPOLEON.

In good truth,
I scarce conceive thee.   What, degenerate
    Rome,
With scarce the power in this strong wind of
    war
To hold her ragged gauds about her limbs ;
Rome, reft of the deep thunder in her voice,
The dark curse in her eye, Rome, old, dumb,
    blind,—
Shall Rome give kingdoms ?—Why, she hath
    already
Transferred her crown to Heaven.

BISHOP.

Canst thou follow
The courses and the genius of the wind,
Father the dark abyss and take wing,

For such as these, is Rome:—the voice of God

Sounding in darkness and a silent place;

The morning dew scarce seen upon the
  flowers,

Yet drawn to heaven and grown the thunder-
  bolt

That strikes a King at noon. When man's
  wild soul

Clutches no more at the white feet of Christ;

When death is not, nor spiritual disease;

When atheists can on the dark mountain
  tops

Walk solitary in the light of stars,

And cry, "God is not;" when no mothers
  kneel

Moaning on graves of children; when no flashes

Trouble the melancholy dark of dream;

When prayer is hush'd, when the Wise Book
  is shut—

Then Rome shall fall **indeed**: meantime she
    is based

Invulnerable on the soul of man,

Its darkest needs and fears; she doth dispense

What soon or late is better prized than gold,--

Comfort and intercession; **for** all sin

She hath the swiftest shrift, wherefore her
    clients

Are those that have sinned deeply, and of such

Is half the dreadful world; **all these** she holds

By that cold **eyeball** which **has read their**
    souls,

So that they look upon **her secretly**

And tremble,—while **in her** dark book of Fate

E'en now she dooms the Teuton.

Enter a MESSENGER.

NAPOLEON.

                    Well, what news?

MESSENGER.

'Tis brief and sad.　The mighty Prussian
　　chiefs,
Gathering their fiery van in silence,
　　close
Toward the imperial City—in whose walls
Treason and Rage and Fear contend together
Like hunger-stricken wolves; and at their
　　cry,
Echoed from Paris to the Vosges, France,
Calling her famish'd children round her
　　knees,
Implores the trembling nations.　All is still,
Like to that silence which precedes the storm,
And shakes the forest leaves without a breath;
But surely as the vaporous storm is woven,
The German closes round the heart of France
His hurricane of lives.

NARDO AND BISHOP.

The ...... thrives
..... the ..... we spake of. (.......
....   Well, speak on !

MESSENGER.

......, like kine that see the gathering
..... clouds,
..... 'neath the shade of rocks and
..... trees,
..... people fly before the sound
..... footsteps, seeking woods
..... , snaring conies for their food,
..... like the beasts ; some fare in
.....
..... the wholesome air, hushing
.....
..... should hear ;

Some scatter west and south, their frighted eyes
Cast backward, with their wretched household
goods;
And where these dwelt, most blest beneath
thy rule,
The German legions thrive, let loose like
swine
Amid the fields of harvest, in their track
Leaving the smoking ruin, and the church
Most desecrated to a sleeping-sty;—
So that the plenteous lands that rolled in gold
Round thine imperial city, lie full bare
To shame, to rapine, to calamity.

NAPOLEON.

O for one hour of empire, that with life
I might consume this sorrow! 'Tis a spell
By which we are subdued!

MESSENGER.

Strasbourg still stands,
Stubborn as granite, but the citadel
Has fallen. Within, Famine and Horror nest,
And rear their young on ruin.   [*Exit.*

Enter a MESSENGER.

NAPOLEON.

How, peal on peal!
Like the agonizing clash of bells, when flame
Has seized on some fair city. News, more
    news!
Dost thou too catch the common trick o' the
    time,
And bring a melancholy peal?

MESSENGER.

My liege,
Strasbourg still stands.

NAPOLEON.

And then?

MESSENGER.

Pent up in Metz,
Encircled by a river of strong lives,
Bazaine is faithful to the cause and thee,
And from his prison doth proclaim himself,
And all the host of Frenchmen at his back,
Thy liegemen to the death.

NAPOLEON.

Why, that last peal
Sounds somewhat blither.   Well?

MESSENGER.

From his lone isle,
The old Italian Red-shirt in his age

Has crawl'd, tho' **sickly** and infirm, to France,
And slowly **there his** leonine **features** breed
Hope in the **timid** people, **who——**

NAPOLEON.

Enough! [*Exit* MESSENGER.
That tune is flat **and tame.**

[*Enter a* MESSENGER.

What man art thou,
On whose swart face **the frenzied lightning
plays,**
Prophetic of the thunder **on the tongue?**
Speak!

MESSENGER.

Better I had died at **Weissemberg,**
Where on the bloody field I lay for dead,

Than live to bring this woe. Ungenerous
      France,

Forgetful of thy gracious years of reign,

Pitiless as a sated harlot is

When ruin overtaketh him whose hand

Hath loaded her with gems, shameless and
      mad,

France, like Delilah, now betrays her lord.

The streets are drunken—from thy palace-gate

They pluck the imperial eagles, trampling
      them

Into the bloody mire ; thy flags and pennons,

Torn from their vantage in the wind, are
      wrapt

In mockery round the beggar's ragged limbs ;

And thine imperial images in stone,

Dash'd from their lofty places, strew the
      ground

In shameful ruin. All the ragged shout,

While from the presidential seat Trochu
Proclaims the empire dead, and calleth up
A new Republic, in whose chairs of office
Thine enemies, scribblers and demagogues,
Simon, Gambetta, Favre, and with these
The miserable Rochefort, trembling grasp
The reins of power, unconscious of the scorn
That doth already doom them.   To their feet
Come humming back, vain-drunken, all the
      wasps
That in thine hour of glory thou didst brush
With careless arm-sweep from thy festal cup :
Shuddering mobs the pigmy Blanc declaims,
The bare-brained Hugo shrieks a maniac song
In concert, and the scribblers, brandishing
Their pens like valiant Lilliputians
Against the Teuton giant, frantically
Scrawl at thee.   Coming with mock humble
      eyes

To the Republic, this sham shape of straw,

This stuff'd thing of a harlot's carnival,

The dilettante sons of Orleans, kneeling,

Proffer forsooth their swords, which, being
    disdain'd,

They sheathe chopfallen, and with bows
    withdraw

Back to their pictures and perfumery.

NAPOLEON.

Why, thine is news indeed.   Nor do I weep

For mine own wrong, but for the woes of
    France,

Whose knell thou soundest.   With a tongue
    of fire

Our enemy shall like the ant-eater

Devour these insect rulers suddenly.

may the foul fiend blacken all
the air

with revolt and fear
the wits of friends and foes,
and with anarchy
fretful councils, till at last,
wild-hair'd, mad, and horrible,
and naked crimson limbs,
Spectre of the Red,
s the shameful knife
; then, in her need,
France shall call
een years of sleep —
rise again.   [

CHORUS.

STROPHE I.

, and making the

Wipe ye the bloody hair out of her beautiful
    eyne,

And cover up her face with the black fold of
    her dress :

Then, lastly, stooping slow, raise her with
    tenderness,

And follow where we lead with a melancholy
    tread,

Beating our baréd breasts to the deep chant
    of the dead ;

Nor fail each man to crave in a deep voice and
    strong,

That God may smite those sore who did her
    this foul wrong ;

Nor fail each man to pause and draw deep
    breaths of prayer,

And all for France, our murdered France,
    whom to the grave we bear.

ANTI-STROPHE I.

Sons, ye are bloody-shod! Sons, ye breathe
    bloody breath!
Your nostrils feel, O sons, the salt sharp
    stench of death!
Your brethren rot afield, your children cry in
    the dark;
Across your sisters' throats the butcher
    leaves his mark;
With shameful finger-stains upon their bosom
    bare,
Your dear ones lie and hide their faces in their
    hair;
And yet I say this night, your pangs are light
    and free
Beside her pangs whose dust ye carry after
    me.

And yet I say this night, hush up your private
wrong,

Gather your wrath, my sons, in one deep
breath and strong—

Curse me the Teuton butchers! Curse me
son, mother, and sire!

Call to the Lord for slaughter! call to the
Lord for fire!

Scream me the thunders down! cry till the
lightnings spring!

And all for France, our mother France, whom
we are carrying.

STROPHE II.

Last night she was a Queen!—draw back the
cloak, and lo!

The pale face set in hair threaded with silver
snow,

The thin close-pressed lips, the delicate silken
chin,

The round great eyes closed up, and dark,
all dark, within.

Come, touch her on the cheek; come, bless
her as she lies;

Come, kiss the dark lids down on the beloved
eyes;

Fall'n in her hour of pride, torn from her
triumph-car,

Is she not dearer still than all things earthly
are?

O France! O Mother! speak. O beautiful
Mother, wake!

Look on us, for we die:—we die for thy dear
sake;

The slayer is at our gates—weak are our
prayers and vain—

. . . Ah, God, she is not dead!—she stirs!
—her eyes unclose again!

ANTI-STROPHE II.

Sons, gather round, gather round! Sons, be
of cheer, be of cheer!

Beautiful, pale as snow, she stirs upon her
bier.

Ah, but she is not dead! Mother, O Mother,
speak!

She rises up her height —the bright blood
burns in her cheek—

See how her great eyes gleam thro' tears of
pain and shame—

See how the mighty lips tremble and quiver
to flame.

She reacheth down to feel her sword, and it is
there—

She holds it up to God; it gleams in the
black air ;

Sons, gather round, gather round! Sons, it
is not too late!

She turns her face to him who croucheth at
the gate—

In the wild wind of war her bloodstain'd gar-
ments wave—

With bitter, bleeding heart, our France springs
up as from the grave.

STROPHE III.

Set the cannon on the heights! and under
Let the black moat gape, the black graves
grow!
Now, let thunder
Answer back the thunder of the foe!
France has torn her cerements asunder—
France doth live, to strike the oppressor
low.

Now let the smithy blaze, and the blue steel
>be sped ;

Twist iron into guns, cast ye the fatal
>lead ;

Drag cannon to the gate,—and let our bravest
>stand

Bare to the shoulder there, smoke-begrim'd,
>torch in hand.

Now to the winds of heaven the Flag of
>Stars upraise ;

Let those sing martial songs who are too frail
>for frays.

France is uprisen again ! France, the sworn
>slayer of Kings !

With bleeding breast and bitter heart, at the
>Teuton's throat she springs.

ANTI-STROPHE III.

Dig the trenches broad and deep! and,
  after,

  They shall serve for foemen's graves as
  well—

Let fierce laughter

  Serve the German butchers for a knell.

Fire the paths they tread! Let floor and
  rafter

  Blaze, till all our city is as Hell.

Now should they enter in, stand ye prepared
  with flame

To light the hidden mine under the city of
  shame.

Gather our children and wives, let them not
  watch or weep;

While we are striking home let them be pray-
  ing deep.

They are famish'd, give them food—they are
    thirsty, let them drink :

Blood shall suffice for us, whether we rise or
    sink.

France is uprisen again!—how should we
    drink and eat,

Till, stiff in death, the Teuton snake is coil'd
    beneath her feet ?

Strophe IV.

Now like thunder
    Be our voice together while we cry—
Kings shall never hold our spirits under,
    Kings shall cast their crowns aside and
        fly.
Latin, Sclav, or Teuton, they shall wonder ;
    The soul of man hath doom'd them--let
        them die.

We have slain Kings of old—they were our
own to slay—

But now we doom all Kings until the Judgment Day.

Raise ye the Flag of Stars! Tremble, O
kings, and behold!

Raise ye the Flag of Man, while the knell of
anarchs is toll'd!

This is a festal day for all the seed of Eve :

France shall redeem the world, and heal all
hearts that grieve ;

France with her sword this day shall free all
human things ;

With blood drain'd from her heart, our France
shall write the doom of Kings.

ANTISTROPHE IV.

Fill each loophole with a man! and finding
Each a foe, aim slowly at the brain,

While the blinding

    Lightnings flash, and the great guns re-

       frain.

To the roofs! and while beneath the foe are

    winding

    Dash ye stones and missiles down like

       rain.

Watch for the greybeard King : to drink his

    blood were great.

Watch for the Cub thereto—aim at his brain

    full straight.

Watch most for that foul Knave, who crawls

    behind the Crown,

Who smiles, befooling all, with crafty eyes

    cast down :

Sweeter than wine indeed his damnëd blood

    would flow,

Curst juggler with our souls, he who hath

    wrought this woe.

France hath aprisen again! Let the fierce

shaft be sped!

Till all the foul Satanic **things that flatter**

Kings be dead!

Strophe V.

Send the light balloon aloft with **singing,**

Let our hopes rise with it to the sky!

Let our voices **like one fount upspringing**

Tell **the mighty realm that hope is**

nigh.

See, in answer, **from the distance wing-**

ing,

Back unto our feet the **swift doves fly.**

Read! read! yes, all **is** well,—yes, let our

hearts be higher;

North, south, east, west, the **souls of** French-

men are afire.

Wildly from hill to hill the blessed tidings
    speed!

Come from your fields, O sons! France is
    arisen indeed.

The reaper leaves the wheat, the workman
    leaves his loom.

Tho' the black priest may frown, who heeds
    his look of gloom?

Flash the wild tidings forth! ring them from
    town to town,—

Till like a storm of scythes we rise, and the
    foe like wheat go down.

ANTI-STROPHE V.

See, how northward the wild heavens lighten!
    Red as blood the fierce aurora waves;
Let it bathe us strong in blood, and brighten
    Sweet with resurrection on our graves—
Lighten, lighten!

Scroll of God! unfold above and brighten!

  Light the doom of monarchs and their

    slaves!

This is a day indeed—be sure that God can

    see.

Raise the fierce cry again, "Liberty!

    Liberty!"

Courage! no man dies twice, and he shall

    live in death,

Who for the Flag of Stars strikes with his

    latest breath.

Nay, not a foe shall live to tell if France be

    slain.

If the wild cause be lost, only the grave shall

    gain.

Teuton and Frank in fierce embrace shall

    strew the fatal sod;

And they shall live indeed who died to save

    their souls for God!

Enter NAPOLEON *and an* OFFICER.

OFFICER.

Once in a dream, being worn and weak, I saw
A fight between a hydra and a wolf,
In which the wily thing, with fold on fold
Of luminous coils enveloping its foe,
So that it could not breathe, nor stir, nor
    scream,
Struck not, but shooting out its hugest
    head,
Coiling it backward as I twist my arm,
Poised o'er the wolf's fierce face, and, with
    red fangs
Drawn and withdrawn to a horrid hissing
    sound,
Gazed stedfast with mesmeric orbs of fire
Into the fierce yet fascinated eyes

That watch'd them slowly closing up for
    doom.

E'en so it seem'd to stand of late with France

And her oppressor. But by God's own
    hand,

Or by some agency well deem'd divine,

The spell is shaken. Screaming in despair

The wolf strikes at the snake, and with
    strong feet

Forcing the horrid head to the ground, pre-
    pares

To spring upon and rend it, though around

The lesser heads, hissing like red-hot iron

Plunged into water, stab, and stab, and
    stab,

With thrusts repeated swift as one can
    breathe,

At the bean sides that run with bitterest
    blood,

While still the great heart throbbeth strong
    and true,
And still the wild face, fearless even to death,
Gleameth by fits with rage and agony.

NAPOLEON.

Is there no hope for France?

OFFICER.

          None. Yet I know not.
A nation thus miraculously strengthen'd,
And acting in the fiercest wrath of love,
Hath risen ere this above calamity,
And out of anguish conjured victory.
If strength and numbers, if the mighty hand
Of the Briareus, shall decide the day,
Then surely as the sun sets France must
    fall;

or prayer a miracle

And bring down to strike for her,

NAPOLEON.

Have we not proved

Yea, by God! Like dogs

the air with wrath upon the

who led and those

friend from foe, while inch by

ranks as a slow fire

or

OFFICER.

Sire——

NAPOLEON.

Why dost thou hang

Thy head, old friend, and look upon the
ground?

Nay, if all Frenchmen had but hearts like
thine,

Then France were blest in sooth, and I, its
master,

Were safe against the swords of all the
world.

OFFICER.

Sire, 'twas not that I meant—my life is yours

To give or take, to blame or praise; I blush'd

Not for myself, but France.

NAPOLEON.

Then hadst thou cause
For crimson cheeks indeed.

OFFICER.

Sire, as I live,
Thou wrongest her! The breast whereon we grew
Suckled no cowards. For one dizzy hour
France totter'd, and look'd back; but now, indeed,
She hath arisen to the very height
Of her great peril.

OFFICER.

Not France betrayed thee, Sire; but rather
    those
Whom thy most noble nature, royally based
Above suspicion and perfidious fear,
Welcom'd unto thy council; not poor France,
Whose bleeding wounds speak for her loud
    as tongues,
Bit at the hand that raised her up so high;
Not France, but bastard Frenchmen, doubly
    damn'd
Alike by her who bare them, and by thee
Who fed them. These betrayed thee to thy
    doom,
And falling clutch'd at thine imperial crown,
Dragging it with them to the bloody dust;
But these that held her arms like bands of
    lead

Being torn from off her, France, unchain'd
  and free,
Uplifts her pale front to the stars, and stand's
Serene in doom and danger, and sublime
In resurrection.

NAPOLEON.

How the popular taint
Corrupts the wholesome matter of thy mind!
This would be treason, friend, if we were
  strong—
Now 'tis less perilous: the commonest wind
Can blow its scorn upon the fallen.

OFFICER.

Sir,
Behold me on my knees, tears in mine eyes,

And sorrow in my heart.   My life is thine,

My life, my heart, my soul are pledged to
    thine ;

And trebly now doth thy calamity

Hold me thy slave and servant.   If I pray,

'Tis that thou mayst arise, and thou shalt rise ;

And if I praise our common mother, France,

Who for the moment hath forgot her lord,

'Tis that my soul rejoices for thy sake,

That, when thou comest to thine own again,

Thy realm shall be a realm regenerate,

Baptised, a fair thing worthy of thy love,

In its own blood of direful victory.

NAPOLEON.

Say'st thou ?—Rise !—Friend, thou art little
    skilled

In reading that abstruse astrology

Whereby our cunning politicians cast

The fate of Kings. France robed in victory,

Is France her ever lost to our great house.

France fallen, is France that with my secret
    hand

I may uplift again. But tell thy tale

Most freely : let thy soul beat its free wings

Before me as it lists. Come! as thou
    sayest,

France is no coward; — she hath at last
    arisen;

Nay, more—she is sublime. Proceed.

OFFICER.

My liege,

God, on he made me thy most loving servant,

Made and baptised me, Frenchman; and my
    heart,

A soldier's heart, yearns out this day in pride

To her who bare me, and both great and low

My brethren.   Courage is a virtue, Sire,

Even in a wretched cause.   In Strasbourg
   still

Old Ulrich, with his weight of seventy years,

Starves unsubdued, while the dull enemy

Look on in wonder at such strength in woe ;

Bazaine still keeps the glittering hosts at
   bay,

And holds them with a watchful hand and
   eye ;

The captain of the citadel of Laon,

Soon as the foeman gather'd on his walls,

Illumed the hidden mine, and Frank and
   Teuton,

With that they strove for, strew'd the path in
   death ;

From Paris to the Vosges, loud and wild,

The tocsin rings to arms, and on the fields

The last ripe ear empties itself unreapt,

While every man whose hand can grasp a
 sword

Flocks to the petty standard of his town.

The many looms of the great factory

Stand silent, but the fiery moulds of clay

Are fashioning cannon, and the blinding
 wheels

Are sharpening steel. In every market-
 place

Peasant and prince are drilling side by
 side ;

Roused from their wine-fed torpor, changed
 from swine

To men, the very country burghers arm,

Nay, what is more to them than blood, bleed
 gold

Bounteously, freely: I have heard that
 priests,

Doffing the holy cassock secretly,

Shouting uplift the sword, and crying Christ

To aid them strike for France.   Only the
basest,

Only the scum, shrink now ; for even women,

Catching the noble fever of the time,

Buckle the war-belts round their lovers'
waists,

And clapping hands, with mingled cries and
sobs,

Urge young and old against the enemy.

NAPOLEON.

Of so much thunder may the lightning spring.

I know how France can thunder, and I have
felt

How women's tongues can urge.   But what
of Paris ?

What of Lutetia? How doth it bear
The terror and the agony?

OFFICER.

Most bravely,
As doth become the glorious heart of France:
Strong, fearless, throbbing with a martial might,
Dispensing from its core the vital heat
Which filleth all the members of the land;
Tho' even now the sharp steel pricks the skin,
To stab it in its strength.

NAPOLEON.

Who holds the reins
Within the gates?

OFFICER.

Trochu.

NAPOLEON.

Still ? Why, how long

Have the poor fools been constant ? Favre

also ?

Gambetta ? Rochefort ? All these gentlemen

Still flourish ? And Thiers ? Hath the arch-

schemer

A seat among the gods, a place of rank

With the ephemera ?

OFFICER.

Not so, my liege.

NAPOLEON.

Well, being seated on Olympus' top,

What thunderbolts are France's puny Joves

Casting abroad? Or do they sit and quake
For awe of their own voices, which in France,
As in the shifting glaciers of the Alps,
May bring the avalanche upon their heads?

OFFICER.

The men, to do them justice, use their power
Calmly and soldierly, and for a time
Forget the bitter humours of the senate
In the great common cause. Paris is strong,
And full of noble souls.

NAPOLEON.

Paris must fall.

OFFICER.

Not soon, my liege; for she is belted round
And armed impregnable on every side.

Hunger and thirst may slay her, not the
    sword;
And ere the foeman's foot is heard within,
Paris will spring upon her funeral pyre
And, boldly as an Indian widow, follow
Freedom, her spouse, to heaven. Last week I
    walk'd
Reading men's faces in the silent streets,
And, as I am a soldier, saw in none
Fear or capitulation : very harlots
Cried in their shame the name of Liberty,
And, hustled from the gates, shriek'd out a
    curse
Upon the coming German : all was still
And dreadful; but the citizens in silence
Drilled in the squares; on the great boulevard
    groups
Whisper'd together, with their faces pale
At white heat; in the silent theatre,

Dim lit by lamps, were women, wives and
    mothers,
Silently working for their wounded sons
And husbands; in the churches, too, they sat
And wrought, while ever and anon a foot
Rung on the pavement, and with sad red eyes
They turn'd to see some armëd citizen
Kneel at his orisons or vespers. Nightly,
Ere the moon rose, the City slept like death;
Yet as a lion sleeps, with half-shut eyes,
Hearing each murmur on the weary wind,
Crouching and steady for the spring. Each
    dawn
I saw the country carts come rumbling in,
And the scared country-folk, with large wild
    eyes
And open mouths, who flock'd for shelter,
    bringing
Horrible tidings of the enemy,

Who had devoured their fields and happy
    homes.
Then suddenly like a low earthquake came
The rumour that the foe was at the gates;
And climbing a cathedral roof that night,
I saw the pitch-black distance sown with fire
Gleam phosphorescent like the midnight sea,
And heard at intervals mysterious sound,
Like far off tempest, or the Atlantic waves
Clashing on some great headland in a storm,
Come smother'd from afar. But, lingering yet,
I haunted the great City in disguise,
While silently the fatal rings were wound
Around about it by the Teuton hosts:
Still, as I am a soldier, saw no face
That look'd capitulation : rather saw
The knitted eyebrow and the clenchéd teeth,
The stealthy hand that fingered with the sword,
The eye that glanced as swift as hunger's doth

Towards the battlements.   Then (for a voice

Was raised against my life) I sought Trochu,

Mine ancient schoolfellow and friend in arms,

And, though his brow darkened a moment's
space,

He knew me faithful, and reached out his hand

To save me.   By his secret help I found

A place in a balloon, that, in the dark

Ere daylight, rose upon a moaning wind,

And drifted southward with the drifting
clouds;

And as the white and frosty daylight grew,

And opening crimson as a rose's leaves

The clouds to eastward parted, I beheld

The imperial City, gables, roofs, and spires,

White and fantastic as a city of dream,

Gleam orient, while the muffled drums within

Sounded reveille; then a flash and wreath

Of vapour broke across the outer line,

Where the black fortifications frowning rose
Ring above ring around the imperial gates,
And flash on flash succeeded with a sound
Most faint and lagging wearily behind.
Still all without the City seemed as husht
As sleep or death. But as the reddening
    day
Scattered the mists, the tiny villages
Loomed dim ; and there were distant glim-
    merings,
And far-off muffled sounds : yet little there
Showed the innumerable enemy,
Who snugly housed and canopied with stone
Lay hidden in their strength ; only the watch-
    fire
Gleam'd here and there, only from place to
    place
Masses of shadow seem'd to move, and
    light

Was glitter'd dimly back from hidden
    steel;

And, wondrous sight of all, miles to the
    west,

Along the dark line of the foe's advance,

On the straight rim where earth and heaven
    meet,

The forests blazed and to the driving clouds

Cast blood-red phantoms growing dim in
    day.

Meantime, like one whirl'd in a dizzy dream,

Onward we drove below the driving cloud,

And from the region of the burning fire

And smouldering hamlet rose still higher, and
    saw

The dim stars like to tapers burning out

Above the region of the nether storm,

And the Blue it self other growing

Silent and dark in the deep wintry dawn.

Enter hastily a MESSENGER.

MESSENGER.

Most weighty news, my liege, from Italy.

NAPOLEON.

Yes?

MESSENGER.

Rome is taken.   The imperial walls
Yawn where the cannon smote; in the red
    streets,
Romans embracing shout for Liberty;
From Florence to Messina bonfires blaze,
And rockets rise and vivas fill the air;
And with the thunder in his aged ears,
Surrounded by his cold-eyed cardinals,

Clutching his spiritual crown more close,

Trembling with dotage, sits the grey-haired

    Pope,

Anathematizing in the Vatican.   [*Exit.*

OFFICER.

Woe to the head on whom his curse shall fall,

For in the day of judgment it shall be

Better with Sodom and Gomorrah.   Wait!

This is the twilight; red will rise the dawn.

NAPOLEON.

Peace, friend; yet if it ease thy heart, speak on.

I would to God, I did believe in God

As thou dost.   Twilight surely—'tis indeed

A twilight, and therein from their fair

    spheres

Kings shoot like stars.　How many nights of
　　late
The heavens have troubled been with fiery
　　signs,
With characters like monstrous hieroglyphs,
And the aurora, brighter than the day
And red as blood, has burnt from west to
　　east.

OFFICER.

I do believe the melancholy air
Is full of pain and portent.

NAPOLEON.

　　　　　　Would to God
I had more faith in God, for in this work
I fail to trace His hand ; but rather feel

The nether-shock of earthquake every where

Shaking old thrones and new, those rear'd on
    rock

As well as those on sand.   All darkens yet,

And in that darkness, while with cheeks of
    snow

The affrighted people gaze at one another,

The Teuton still, mouthing of Deity,

Works steadfastly to some mysterious end.

My heart was never Rome's so much as
    now,

Now, when she shares my cup of agony.

Agony!   Is this agony? then, indeed,

All life is agony.

OFFICER.

            Your Imperial Highness

Is suffering?   Take comfort, Sire.

NAPOLEON.

It is nought—
Only a passing spasm at the heart—
'Tis my disease, comrade; 'tis my disease!
So leave me: it is late; and I would rest.

OFFICER.

God in his gracious goodness give thee health.

NAPOLEON.

Pray that He may; for am I deeply sick—
Too sick for surgery—too sick for drugs—
Too sick for man to heal.   'Tis a complaint
Incident to our house; and of the same
Mine imperial uncle died.   [*Exit Officer.*
France in the dust,
With the dark Spectre of the Red above her!

Rome fallen! Aye me, well may the face of
  heaven
Burn like a fiery scroll. Had I but eyes
To read whose name is written next for doom!
The Teuton's? O the Serpent, that has bided
His time so long, and now has stabbed so deep!
Would I might bruise his head before I die!
                                      [*Exit.*

Night. NAPOLEON *sleeping.* *Chorus of*
                    SPIRITS.

A VOICE.

What shapes are ye whose shades darken his
    rest this night?

CHORUS.

Cold from the grave we come, out of the dark
    to the light.

A Voice.

Voices ye have that moan, and eyes ye have
    that weep.
Ah, woe for him who feels such shadows
    round his sleep!

Chorus.

Tho' thou wert buried and dead, still would
    we seek and find thee,
Fly where thou wilt, thou shalt hear feet from
    the tomb behind thee.
Sleep? shall thy soul have sleep? Nay, but
    it shall be shaken.
Gather around him there, spirits of earth and
    air, trouble him till he awaken!

A Voice.

Who in imperial raiment, darkly frowning,
    stand,
Laurel-leaves in their hair, sceptred, yet sword
    in hand?

Another Voice.

Who in their shadow looms, woman-eyed,
    woe-begone,
And bares his breast to show the piteous
    wounds thereon?

Chorus.

Peace, they are kings; they are crown'd;
    kings, tho' their realms have departed;
Realms of the grave they have, and they walk
    in the same weary-hearted.

Sleep? Did their souls have sleep? Nay, for
    like his was their being.
Gather around him there, spirits of earth and
    air, wake him to hearing and seeing.

SPIRIT OF HORTENSE.

Woe! O ye shades unblest,
Leave ye my child to rest,
    Leave me here weeping.
This night, at least, have grace,
See, the poor weary face
    Child-like in sleeping.

SPIRIT OF CÆSAR.

Greater than thou, I fell: thy day is o'er.
Thou reap the world with swords! thou wear
    the robe I wore!

Back to the books and read again how, in his

    hour of pride,

At the foot of Pompey's statue, slain by slaves,

    Imperial Cæsar died.

SPIRIT OF HORTENSE.

  Woe! From his bed depart,

  Ye who first taught his heart

    Bloody ambition.

  Back! he is God's in sleep:

  Ah, in his heart burn deep

    Pain and contrition.

SPIRIT OF BONAPARTE.

Greater than thou! I will die, and give place.

Thou take from my cold grave the glory and

  the grave!

Thou rise victorious where I fell!   Back to
    thy books, thou blind!
Read how I watch'd the weary Sea, less vast
    than my imperial mind.

NAPOLEON (*in sleep*).

Dost thou too frown, dark Spirit of our
    house?
Scorn be thy meed for scorn.   Thou hadst
    become
A theme for nameless bards, a lullaby
For country folk to rock their cradles with,
A sound, a voice, an echo of a name
Dying most melancholy.   In my mouth
Thy name became a trumpet once again,
And woods and wilds, to earth's remotest
    peaks,
Echoed "Napoleon."   Cursed be the name,

Cursed be thou, this day! . . . O mother!
mother!

SPIRIT OF HORTENSE.

Father in Heaven, they rise!—
Spirits with dreadful eyes
    Hither are creeping.
Thrice on his brow I write
Thy blessed Cross this night,
    Mourning and weeping.

A VOICE.

What spirit art thou, with cold still smile and
horrible brow?

SPIRIT.

Orphan, and avenged. Too soon I struck the
blow.

A VOICE.

And thou, with bloody breast, and eyes that
    roll in pain?

SPIRIT.

I am that Maximilian, miserably slain.

A VOICE.

And ye, O shadowy things, featureless, wild,
    and stark?

CHORUS.

We are the nameless ones whom he hath
    slain in the dark!

A VOICE.

Ye whom this man hath doom'd, Spirits, are
ye all there?

CHORUS.

Not yet; we come, we come—we darken all
the air.

A VOICE.

O latest come, and what are ye? Why do ye
moan and call?

CHORUS.

O hush! O hush! we come to speak the
bitterest curse of all.

HORTENSE.

Woe!—for the spirits wild,
Woman and man and child,

Hither are creeping.
Thrice on his brow I write
Thy blessed Cross this night,
Moaning and weeping.

CHORUS.

Ours is the bitterest curse of all ;—for we
Are Souls that perish'd, foully slain by thee.
Ah! would that thou hadst slain our bodies
    too, like theirs!
We ate of shame and sorrow till we ceased,
We drank all poisonous things at thy foul
    feast—
Back from the grave we come, with curses
    deep, not prayers.

With Sin and Death our mothers' milk was
    sour,
The womb wherein we grew from hour to hour

Gather'd pollution dark from the polluted
    frame—
  Beside our cradles naked Infamy
  Caroused, and Lust sat smiling hideously—
We grew like evil weeds apace, and knew not
    shame.

  With incantations and with spells most
    rank,
  The fount of Knowledge where we might
    have drank,
And learnt to love the taste, was hidden from
    our eyes;
  And if we learn'd to spell out written
    speech,
  Thy slaves were by, and we had books to
    teach
Falsehood and Filth and Sin, Blasphemies,
    Scoffs, and Lies.

We drank of poison, ev'n as flowers drink
    dew;
We ate and drank of poison till we grew
Noxious, polluted, black, like that whereon
    we fed;
  We never felt the light and the free wind—
  Sunless we grew, and deaf, and dumb, and
    blind—
How should we dream of God, souls that were
    slain and dead?

  Love, with her sister Reverence, passed
    our way
As angels pass, unseen, but did not stay—
We had no happy homes wherein to bid them
    dwell;
  We turn'd from God's blue heaven with
    eyes of beast,

We heard alike the atheist and the priest,
And both these lied alike to smooth our
    hearts for Hell.

Of some, both Soul and Body died; of
    most,
The Body fatten'd on, while the poor ghost,
Prison'd from the sweet day, was withering
    in woe;
Some robed in purple quaff'd their fatal
    cup,
Some out of rubied goblets drank it up—
We did not know God was; but now, O God,
    we know.

Ah woe, ah woe, for those thy sceptre
    sway'd,
Woe most for those whose bodies, fair
    array'd,

Insolent, sat at ease, smiled at thy feet of
    pride;
  Woe for the harlots, with their painted
    bliss!
Woe for the red wine-oozing lips they kiss!
Woe for the Bodies that lived, woe for the
    Souls that died!

  Lambs of thy flock, but oh! not white and
    fair;
  Beasts of the field, tamed to thy hand, we
    were;
Not men and women—nay, not heirs to light
    and truth:
  Some fattening, ate and fed; some lay at
    ease;
  Some fell and linger'd of a long disease;
But all look'd on the ground—beasts of the
    field forsooth.

It is too late—it is too late this night—

To bid us live again in the fair light;

Back from the grave we come, with curses

deep, not prayers.

Ours is a darker doom than theirs, who died

Strewing with blood the pathway of thy

pride—

Ah, would that thou hadst slain our bodies

too, like theirs!

SEMI-CHORUS I.

Tho' thou wert buried and dead, still would

they seek thee and find thee.

Fly where thou wilt thou shalt hear feet from

the grave behind thee.

HORTENSE.

Woe! woe! woe!

SEMI-CHORUS II.

Ye who beheld dim light thro' the chink of
the dungeon gleaming,

And watch'd your shade on the wall, till it
took a sad friend's seeming ;

Ye who in dark disguise fled from the doom
and the danger,

And dragging a patriot's chain died in the
land of the stranger.

Men whom he set aside to die like beasts in
the traces !

Women he set aside for the trade of polluting
embraces !

Say, shall his soul have sleep? or shall it be
darken'd and shaken ?

CHORUS.

Gather around him there, spirits of earth and
air, trouble him till he awaken.

NAPOLEON *is waking*.

Who's there? Who speaks?—All silent. O
    how slowly
Moveth the dark and melancholy night.
I cannot rest—I am heart-sick at heart—
I have had ill dreams. The inevitable
    Eyes
Are watching, and the weary void of sleep
His voices strangely seal.
             He rises, and paces the chamber.

              O those dark years
Of Empire! He who tames the tiger, and
    lies
Pillows his perilous neck in a lone cave,
I ask—Who could sleep on such a bed?
Mine eyes were ever dry of the sweet dew

God scatters on the lids of happy men ;

Watching with fascinated gaze the orbs,

Ring within ring of blank and bestial light,

Where the wild fury slept : seeking all arts

To soothe the savage instinct in its throes

Of passionate unrest ; with one hand holding

Sweet things within my palm for it to lap,

And with the other, held behind my back,

Clutching the secret steel : oft, lest the thing

Should fasten on its master, cunningly

Turning its wrath against the shapes that moved

Outside its splendid lair ; until at last,

Let forth to the mad light of War, it sprang

Shrieking, and sought to rend me. O thou beast !

Art thou so wild this day ? and dost thou thirst

To fix on thine imperial ruler's throat ?

Why, I have bidden thee "down," and thou
    hast crouch'd,
Tamely as any hound! Thou shalt crouch yet,
And bleed with shamefuller stripes!

                 Let me be calm,
Not bitter. 'Tis too late for bitterness.
Yet I could gnaw my heart to think how
    France
Hath kill'd me! nay, not France, but rather
    those
Whom to high offices and noble seats
In France's name I raised. I bought their
    souls—
What soul can power not buy?—and, having
    lost
The blessed measure of all human truth,
Being soulless, these betrayed me; yea,
    became

A brood of lesser tigers, hungering

With their large eyes on mine. I did not
    build

My throne on sand; no, no,—on Lies and
    Liars,

Weaker than sand a thousandfold!

                          In this

I did not work for evil. Though my means

Were dark and vile perchance, the end I
    sought

Was France's weal, and underneath my care

She grew as tame as any fatted calf.

I never did believe in that stale cry

Raised by the newsman and the demagogue,

Tho' for mine ends I could cry " Liberty !"

As loud as any man. The draff of men

Are as mere sheep and kine, with heads held
    down

Grazing, or resting blankly ruminant.

These must be tended, must be shepherded,

But Frenchmen are as wild things scarcely
    tamed,

Brute-like yet fierce, mad too with some few
    hours

Of rushing freely with an angry roar.

These must be awed and driven.   By a
    scourge

Dripping with sanguine drops of their own
    blood,

I awed them : then I drove them : then in time

I tamed them.   Fool! deeming them wholly
    mine,

I sought to snatch a little brief repose ;

But with a groan they found me, and I woke ;

And, since they seemed to suffer pain, I said,

"Loosen the yoke a little," and 'twas done,

And they could raise their heads and gaze at
    me;

And the wild hunger deepen'd in their eyes,

While fascinated on my throne I sat,

Forcing a melancholy smile of peace.

O had I held the scourge in my right hand!

Tighten'd the yoke instead of loosening !

It had not been so ill with me as now.

But Pity found me with her sister Fear,

And lured me.   He who sitteth on a throne

Should have no counsellers who come in
    tears ;

But rather that still voice within his brain,

Imperturbable as his own cold eyes,

And viewless as his coldly flowing blood ;

Rather a heart as strong as the great heart

Driving the hot blood thro' a lion's thews ;

Rather a will that moves to its desire

As steadfast as the silent-footed cloud.

What peevish humour did my mother mix

With that important ichor of our race

Which, unpolluted, filled mine uncle's veins?

He lash'd the world's Kings to his triumph-

    car,

And sat like marble while the fiery wheels

Dript blood beneath him : tho' the live earth

    shriek'd

Below him, he was calm, and, like a god,

Cold to the eloquence of human tears,

Cold to the quick, cold as the light of stars,

Cold as the hand of Death on the damp

    brow,

Cold as Death brooding on a battle-field

In the white horse-dawn,—from west to east,

Regal he moved as the red wintry sun.

He never flatter'd Folly at his feet :

He never sought to syrup Infamy ;

He, when the martyrs curst him, drew around

    him

The purple of his glory, and passed on

Indifferently, like Olympian Jove.

There was no weak place in the steel he
    wore,

Where woman's tongues might reach his
    mighty heart

As they have reach'd at mine.   O had I kept

A heart of steel, a heart of adamant;

Had I been deaf to clamour and the peal

Of peevish fools; had I for one strong hour

Conjured mine uncle's soul to mix with
    mine,

Sedan had never slain me!   I am lost

By the damn'd implements mine own hands
    wrought—

Things that were made as slavish tools of
    peace,

Never as glittering weapons meet for war.

He never stoop'd to use such peaceful tools!

But, for all uses,

Made the sword serve him—yea, for sceptre
    and scythe;
Nay more, for Scripture and for counsellor.

Yet he too fell. Early or late, all fall.
No fruit can hang for ever on the tree.
Daily the tyrant and the martyr meet
Naked at Death's door, with the fatal mark,
Both brows being branded. Doth the world
    then slay
Only its anarchs? Doth the lightning flash
Smite Cæsar and spare Brutus? Nay, by
    heaven!
Rather the world keeps for its paracletes
Tortures more subtle and more piteous doom
Than it dispenses to its torturers.
Tiberius, with his foot on the world's neck,
Smileth his cruel smile and groweth gray,
Half dead already with the weight of years,

Drinketh the death he is too frail to feel,

While in his noon of life the Man Divine

Hath died in anguish at Jerusalem.

[*He opens a Life of Jesus and reads. A long pause.*

Here too the Teuton works, crafty and slow,

Anatomizing, gauging, questioning,

Till that fair Presence which redeem'd the
        world

Dwindles into a phantom and a name.

Shall he slay Kings, and spare the King of
        Kings ?

In her fierce madness, France denied her God;

But the still Teuton doth destroy his God,

Coldly as he outwits an enemy.

Yet doth he keep the name upon his lips,

And, coldly dedicating the dull deed

To the abstraction he hath christen'd God,

To the creation of his cogent brain,

Conjures against the blessed Nazarene,

That pallid apparition masculine,

That shining orb hemm'd in with clouds of
    flesh ;

Till, darken'd with the woe of his own words,

The fool can turn to Wilhelm's wooden face

And Bismarck's crafty eyes, and see therein

Human regeneration, or at least

The Teuton's triumph mightier than Christ's.

Lie there, Iconoclast!   Thou art thrice a fool,

Who, having nought to set within its place

But civic doctrine and a naked sword,

Would tear from out its niche the piteous bust

Of Him whose face was Freedom's morning
    star.

           [*Takes up a second Book, and reads.*

Mark, now, how speciously Theology,

Leaving the broken fragments of the Life

Where the dull Teuton's hand hath scatter'd
    them,
Takes up the cause in her high fields of air.
"Darkness had lain upon the earth like blood,
And in the darkness human things had
    shriek'd
And felt for God's soft hand, and agonised.
But, overhead, the awful Spirit heard
Yet stirred not, on His throne. Then lastly,
    One
Dropt like a meteor stone from suns afar,
And stirred and stretch'd out hands, and lived,
    and knew
That He indeed had dropt from suns afar,
That He had fallen from the Father's breast,
Where He had slumber'd for eternities;
Hither in likeness of a man He came—
He, Jesus, wander'd forth from heaven and
    said,

"'Lo, I, the deathless one, will live and die!
Evil must suffer—Good ordains to suffer—
Our point of contact shall be suffering,
There will we meet, and ye will hear my
    voice;
And my low voice shall echo on thro' time,
And one salvation, proved in bloody tears,
Be the salvation of humanity.'"

Ah, old Theology, thou strikest home!
"Evil *must* suffer—Good *ordains* to suffer"—
Say'st thou? Did He then quaff His cup of
    tears
Freely, who might have dash'd it down, and
    rul'd?
His world was ready with an earthly crown,
And yet He wore it not. Ah, He was wise!
Had He but sat upon a human throne,
With all the kingdom's beggars at His feet,

And all its coffers open at His side,

He had died more shameful death, yea, He
    had fallen

Even as the Cæsars. Rule the world with
    Love?

Tame savage human nature with a kiss?

Turn royal cheeks for the brute mob to smite?

He knew men better, and He drew aside,

Ordain'd to do and suffer, not to reign.

My good physician bade me search in books

For solace. Can I find it? Verily,

From every page of all man's hand hath
    writ

A dark face frowns, a voice moans " Vanity!"

There is one Book—one only--that for ever

Passeth the understanding and appeaseth

The miserable hunger of the heart—

Behold it—written with the light of stars
By God in the beginning.

[*Looks forth.* A starry night.

                                    I believe
God is, but more I know not, save but this,
He passeth not as men and systems pass,
For while all change, the Law by which they
        change
Survives, and is for ever, being God.
Our sin, our loss, our misery, our death,
Are but the shadows of a dream: the hum
Within our ears, the motes within our eyes;
Death is to us a semblance and an end,
But is as nothing to that central Law
Whereby we cannot die.

                                Yonder blue dome,
Gleaming with meanings mystically wrought,
Hath been from the beginning, and shall be

Until the end.   How many awe-struck eyes
Have look'd and spelt one word—the name of
 God,
And call'd it as they listed, Law, Fate, Change,
And marvell'd for its meaning till they died;
And others came and stood upon their graves,
And read the same, and marvelling too, gave
 place.
The Kings of Israel watch'd it with wild orbs,
Madden'd, and cried the Name, and drew the
 sword.
Above the tented plain of Troy it bent
After the sun of day had set in blood.
The superstitious Roman look'd by night
And trembled.   All these faded phantom-
 like,
And lo! where it remaineth, watch'd with
 eyes
As sad as any of those this autumn night,—

The Higher Law writ with the light of Stars
By God in the beginning . . .

                Let me sleep!
Or I shall gaze and gaze till I grow wild,
And never sleep again.   Too much of God
Maketh the heart sick.   Come then forth, thou
    charm,
Thou silent spell wrung from the blood-red
    flower,
With power to draw the curtains of the soul
And shut the inevitable Eyes away.

    [Drinks a sleeping draught and lies down.

O mother, at thy knees I said a prayer—
Lead me not into temptation, and, O God,
Deliver me from evil.   Is it too late
To murmur it this night?   This night, O
    God,
Whate'er Thou art and wheresoe'er Thou art,

This night at least, when I am sick and fallen,
Deliver me from evil!

[He sleeps.

Chorus of Citizens.

O thou with features dire,
Who crouchest at our gates this bloody day,
  With God's Name on thy forehead burnt in
    fire,
What art thou?   Speak, and say!
  What is thy kindred, monster?   Who thy
    sire?
Whose word wilt thou obey?
  God never made so black a thing as
    thou,
  God never wrote that name upon thy
    brow;
Thou art too foul for God, to whom we
  pray.

Fatal thou broodest on our hearths, with eyes
    Glazed in hunger only blood can sate.
    Begone!—within our breasts the sick heart
        dies
    To see thee crouch and wait :
O blasphemy of nature, at our cries
    God cometh soon or late.
Famine, and Thirst, and Horror at thy back
Lie moaning; Fire and Ruin mark thy track ;
    Begone, and die, thou thing of Sin and
        Hate !
    Die now, ere once again
    The sharp sob of the slain
Goes up the azure voids, and knocks at
    Heaven's Gate.

CHORUS.

    Christ shall arise.
    Power and its vanity,

K

Pride's black insanity,

Lust and its revelry,

Shall, with war's devilry,

Pass from humanity :

Christ shall arise.

SEMI-CHORUS I.

Kings shall pass like shadows from His
whiteness,
Swords be turn'd to scythes and reap the
wheat.

SEMI-CHORUS II.

Slaves that crawl'd round thrones shall fear
His brightness,
Thrones shall be as dust around His
feet.

CHORUS OF CITIZENS.

How long, O Lord, how long,

Shall we linger, frail and feeble as we
    are?

   Thou art slow who shouldst be swift to
      right our wrong,

   Thou wert promised in our very cradle
      song:

Thou hast come and gone above us like a
      Star!

   'Tis a story of old times that Thou art
      strong;

But Thou comest not, Thou comest not from
      far:

   And the cruel fall upon us in their throng,—

And we bleed beneath the tramping feet of
      War.

SEMI-CHORUS I.

Peace! He shall arise; be dumb and duteous;
  Listen, hush your wild hearts, and be wise.

SEMI-CHORUS II.

Sin shall look and die: He is so beauteous;
  Make your spirits pure to bear His eyes.

CHORUS OF THE DEAD.

Where we sleeping lie, where we sleeping lie,
We hear the sound, and our spirits cry;
As we sleeping lie in the Lord's own Breast,
Calm, so calm, for the place is blest,
We, who died that this might be,
Souls of the great, and wise, and free;

Souls that sung, and souls that sighed,

Souls that pointed to God and died ;

Souls of martyrs, souls of the wise ;

Souls of women with weeping eyes ;

Souls whose graves like waves of the sea

  Cover the world from west to east ;

Souls whose bodies ached painfully,

  Till they broke 'to prophetic moan and

  ceased ;

Souls that sleep in the gentle night,

We hear the cry and we see the light.

Did we die in vain ? did we die in vain ?

Ah ! that indeed were the bitterest pain !

But no, but no, 'twere a Father's guilt

If a drop of our blood was vainly spilt.

Not a life, nay, not a breath,

But killed some shape of terror and death ;—

And we see the light and we bless the cry,

Where we sleeping lie, where we sleeping lie.

Semi-Chorus I.

Blest are ye who followed Him and feared not,
　　Yea, into the dark shadow of the tomb !

Semi-Chorus II.

Woe for those who saw ye and revered not ;
　　Better they were formless in the womb !

Chorus.

　　Christ shall arise.
　　Scorning all vanity,
　　Sweetness and sanity,
　　Meekness and lowliness,
　　Shall to love's holiness
　　Shepherd humanity.
　　Christ shall arise.

CHORUS OF CITIZENS.

He cometh late, this God!

Promised for countless years, He cometh late.

Where shall He dwell? The cities of our
state

Are level with the sod.

Shall He upbuild them then? Meantime we
wait,

And see black footsteps where our martyrs trod.

He cometh late, forsooth He cometh late,

This promised Lord our God!

Nor do we see the earth that He will claim,

Is riper yet than when He went away.

There are more ruins only, and the same

Are multiplied each day.

All lands are bloody, and a crimson flame

Eats Hope's poor heart away.

Where shall we turn for peace? whom shall
    we trust for stay?
The anarchs of the world still sit and sway
The hearts of men to evil;—Hunger and
    Thirst
Moan at the palace door; and birds of
    prey
Still scream above the harvest as at first.
    Should He then come at all,˙
    This God on whom ye call,
How should He dwell on earth? would He
    not find it curst?

SEMI-CHORUS I.

Nay, for the Lamb shall wrap the world in
    whiteness;
  Nay, for the wise shall make it fair and
    sweet.

Slaves and fools shall perish in the bright-
    ness!
Thrones shall be as dust around His feet!

SEMI-CHORUS II.

Peace! ye make a useless lamentation.
    Peace! ye wring your hands o'er things of
        stone.
Comfort! ye shall find a habitation
    Fairer than the fairest overthrown.

FINAL CHORUS, OR EPODE.

    Comfort, O true and free,
    Soon shall there rise for ye
A city fairer far than all ye plan;
    Built on a rock of strength,
    It shall arise at length,
Stately and fair and vast, the city meet for
        man!

Towering to yonder skies,
Shall the fair City rise,
In the sweet dawning of a day more pure :
House, mart, and street and square,
Yea, and a Fane for prayer,
Fair, and yet built by hands, strong, for it
    shall endure.

In the fair City then,
Shall walk white-robëd men,
Wash'd in the river of peace that watereth it;
Woman with man shall meet
Freely in mart and street,
At the great council-board woman with man
    shall sit.

Hunger and Thirst and Sin
Shall never pass therein ;

Fed with pure dews of love, children shall

    grow;

    Nought shall be bought and sold,

    Nought shall be given for gold,

All shall be bright as day, all shall be white

    as snow.

    There, on the fields around,

    All men shall till the ground,

Corn shall wave yellow, and bright rivers

    stream;

    Daily, at set of sun,

    All, when their work is done,

Shall watch the heavens yearn down and the

    strange starlight gleam.

    In the fair City of men,

    All shall be silent then,

While on a reverent lute, gentle and low,

    Some holy Bard shall play

Ditties divine, and say
Whence those that hear have come, whither
in time they go.

No man of blood shall dare
Wear the white mantle there;
No man of lust shall walk in street or mart;
Yet shall the magdalen
Walk with the citizen;
Yet shall the sinner grow gracious and pure of
heart.

Now, while days come and go,
Doth the fair City grow,
Surely its stones are laid in sun and moon.
Wise men and pure prepare
Ever this City fair.
Comfort, O ye that weep: it shall arise full
soon.

When, stately, fair, and vast,
  It doth uprise at last,
Who shall be King thereof, say, O ye wise :—
    When the last blood is spilt,
    When the fair City is built,
Unto the throne thereof, a Monarch shall
      arise.

  Hearken, O pure and free,
  When 'tis upbuilt for ye,
Out of the grave He shall arise again ;
    He whose blest soul did plan
    This the fair CITY of MAN,
In his white robes of peace, CHRIST shall
      arise, and reign.